LITTLE MONSTER'S COUNTING BOOK

by Mercer Mayer

to
Cassandra

MERRIGOLD PRESS • NEW YORK

1 one

One is one box
of popcorn.

Mr. Grithix shares some with Little Laff.

2 two

Two is two lollipops.

Little Laff gives one lollipop to Mr. Grithix.
How many lollipops does Little Laff have now?

3 three

Three is three Trollusks with three hats.
How many flags do they have?

How many bow ties are they wearing?

4 four

Four is four legs and four feet
and four spots on his back.

How many horns are there on his nose?

5 five

OOOOO

Five is...

five fingers

five fingers

five toes

five toes

How many teeth does he have?

6 six

Six is six stamps, stuck on the
Stamp-Collecting Trollusk.

How many stamps have fallen to the ground?

7 seven

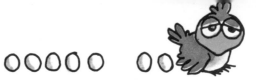

Seven is seven little devils, bundled up in bed.

How many pointed tails can you see?
How many little devils are happy?

8 eight

Eight is eight ice cream cones.

One cone fell on his head. How many are left?

9 nine

Nine is nine squares in the
dust, drawn by Suzy Bombanat.
She likes to play hopscotch.

How many squares have a rock on them?

10 ten

Ten is ten letters on the chalk board.
Little Monster drew them there.

How many letters are right?

10 Ten little Weedles
Sitting in a row;
If one falls down,
How many to go?

9 Nine little Weedles
Sitting in a row;
If one falls down,
How many to go?

8 Eight little Weedles
Sitting in a row;
If one falls down,
How many to go?

7 Seven little Weedles
Sitting in a row;
If one falls down,
How many to go?

6 Six little Weedles
Sitting in a row;
If one falls down,
How many to go?

5 Five little Weedles
Sitting in a row;
If one falls down,
How many to go?

4 Four little Weedles
Sitting in a row;
If one falls down,
How many to go?

3 Three little Weedles
Sitting in a row;
If one falls down,
How many to go?

2 Two little Weedles
Sitting in a row;
If one falls down,
How many to go?

1 One little Weedle
Sitting with a frown
'Cause he's all alone—
The rest are on the
ground.

11 eleven

Eleven is eleven letters, being delivered by the Mail Trollusk. Right now, he is putting a letter in a mailbox.

How many letters are left in his bag?

12 twelve

Twelve is twelve apples, just a snack for a Yalapappus.

How many apples are red and ripe?

13 thirteen

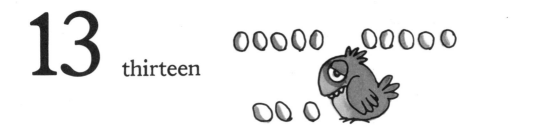

Thirteen is thirteen cookie jars.

How many are open?

14

fourteen

Fourteen is the fourteen hairs
left on Mr. Quandrey's head.

How many are on the floor?

15 fifteen

Fifteen is the fifteen arrows Ms. Errg shot at the target.

She is a marksmonster, but she only hit the bull's-eye once.
How many times did she miss the bull's-eye?

16 sixteen

Sixteen is sixteen fish.

Little Monster caught one. How many fish
are left in the lake?

17 seventeen

Seventeen is seventeen sunflowers in Professor Wormbog's garden.

How many have grown nice and tall?

18

eighteen

Eighteen is eighteen rabbits.
Little Monster made them appear
by a magic trick.

How many have jumped out of the hat?

19

nineteen

Nineteen is nineteen books,
and they all belong to Little Monster.

The one he is reading is open. How many are closed?

20 twenty

Twenty is twenty shoes, made today
by Mr. Grithix, the shoemaker.

How many are on the shelf?

Twenty-one is twenty-one marbles.

How many marbles are in the circle?
How many marbles are red?
How many are orange?
How many are yellow?
How many are green?
How many are blue?
How many are purple?